Out of Orbit

Carole Wilkinson

Published by Sundance Publishing
P.O. Box 1326, 234 Taylor Street, Littleton, MA 01460

Copyright © text Carole Wilkinson

First published 1999 as Phenomena by
Horwitz Martin
A Division of Horwitz Publications Pty Ltd
55 Chandos St., St. Leonards NSW 2065 Australia

Exclusive United States Distribution: Sundance Publishing

ISBN 0-7608-4948-X

Printed in Canada

Contents

Author's Note

I wanted this story to be something that might be possible in the next hundred years. I picked Alpha Centauri as the location of the story because it is the closest solar system to ours. If humans do achieve space travel near the speed of light, this is probably where they will go.

No one knows if there are any planets in the Alpha Centauri system, or what they would be like. I therefore had great fun inventing a planetary system. As there are two suns orbiting each other, I made it different from our solar system. Alpha Centauri A and B are similar in size to our sun. Some scientists think it is quite possible that there would be life on planets orbiting them. I decided to have one planet where there is only plant life.

Carole Wilkinson was once a laboratory technician. She decided that wasn't much fun and now writes books for children and teenagers instead.

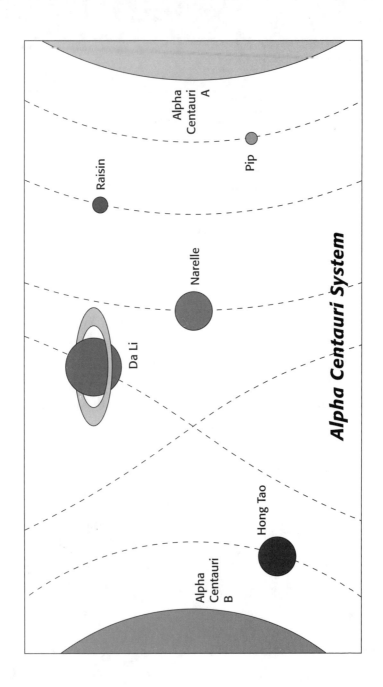

Alpha Centauri A

Pip

Raisin

Narelle

Da Li

Hong Tao

Alpha Centauri B

Alpha Centauri System

Chapter 1
Blindfold

<u>Fact</u>: Radiation is the transmission of energy through space. Some forms of radiation are harmful to humans

Being in the shield room was like wearing a blindfold. On the other side of its blank, metallic walls, anything could be happening. That was the whole point of the shield room: nothing could get in—no light, no sound, no radiation. Juliana looked at her watch. They had been there for five hours.

It happened around lunchtime. She had just been thinking about making a sandwich when her father had hustled her into the shield room with the other kids. There were solar flares, not an unusual occurrence in this part of the universe. This time, both suns were flaring at the same moment.

"What about you?" Juliana had asked as her father gave her a quick kiss.

> **solar flare**: A violent eruption of gas on the sun's surface.

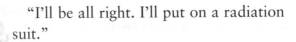

"I'll be all right. I'll put on a radiation suit."

The effects of radiation accumulated. Juliana knew that. It was important that children weren't exposed to it. But a small amount of radiation probably wouldn't harm adults.

Though she never had the chance to make her sandwich, Juliana's appetite had disappeared. If only she knew what was happening outside. The computer screen in the shield room had gone blank two hours ago. That's what solar flares could do— blow out computer systems and wreck radio transmitters/receivers, or transceivers.

Juliana looked around at the others. Sage, the oldest, was playing a game. Did he ever do anything else? He usually spent most of his waking life hidden behind a games mask. The mask projected three-dimensional images to make the players feel as if they were actually in the game. Sage had brought his mask into the shield room. But it had blown at the same time as the computers. He was using his battery-operated wristpad instead.

He was trying to look cool and relaxed, so he wouldn't frighten the younger ones. But Juliana could tell he was nervous. He was only on the third level of his favorite war game. Already he'd lost half his army and six tanks. That was pretty unusual for Sage.

Bogdan had been accessing information about the chemical structure of the planet Da Li when his computer blew. He was only comfortable when he was looking at a screen. The real world made him uneasy. He was still staring at the blank screen.

"How long can solar flares last, Bogdan?" Juliana asked. The only time she ever spoke to him was if she wanted information. He was a walking database.

"The longest recorded solar flare in this system was two hours, forty-five minutes, and thirty-five seconds. There's never been a double flare in recorded history."

Perhaps a double flare could last for five hours. But that seemed like a long time.

Diona started hammering angrily on the hatch. She'd been doing that about every half hour—in between redoing her hair and her nails.

Diona acted like a teenager. She was actually just a nine-year-old spoiled brat.

"You're the worst parents in the history of the universe," she yelled at the hatch. "If you don't let me out immediately, I'm going to report you to the . . ." She stopped for a moment and turned to Bogdan. "What's that organization that punishes bad parents?"

"IRFAC," said Bogdan, still staring at the blank screen. "International Rights For All Children."

"Oh, yeah." She continued yelling. "I'll report you to the IRFAC. They'll throw you in jail."

Diona took everything personally. It hadn't occurred to her that her parents might be in danger.

Astrid was asleep with her head in Sage's lap. That was one thing to be grateful for. She'd been playing with an annoying voice-activated toy for hours. When she made sounds, it would play various tunes.

They were on the space station *Providus*, which had arrived in the Alpha Centauri system five years before. Alpha Centauri was 4.35 light-years from Earth. Juliana was only five when they had left Earth. She

> **light-year**: The distance that light travels in one year in a vacuum—5.88 trillion miles.

was a month short of ten when they arrived. She could hardly remember Earth. The only world she'd ever known was the *Providus*.

Alpha Centauri was a triple star system with five planets. Her father was part of a small scientific team studying one of those planets, Narelle. It was the only planet ever discovered that had an atmosphere similar to Earth's.

It had oxygen—not quite enough, though. Humans could breathe the air, but after a while they got a sickness similar to altitude sickness.

It had water—more than they needed. The driest parts of the planet were ankle deep in water. Flash floods happened all the time.

The other big thing about Narelle was that it had life. Not animal life, but plant life. In fact, it was overrun with plants. That's what her father was interested in. That's why they'd traveled across the universe.

Juliana looked at her watch again. Five and a half hours. She had a splitting headache. But worse than that was the feeling of dread in her stomach. Something was wrong, she knew it. Even if there was the worst radiation ever known, her father would have found the time to let her know that he was all right.

The other children were all members of one family, though you would never know it. They all looked different. And they didn't seem to like each other much. Their father was a famous Japanese astronomer. Sage's Australian mother had died when he was a baby. His father had remarried. His current wife, Diona and Astrid's mother, was African. Bogdan was a refugee from one of the New European conflicts. They had adopted him before they left Earth.

Diona took a break from shouting at her parents. Sage walked over to the hatch. He started to play with the keypad on the wall next to the hatch.

"What do you think you're doing?" said Bogdan.

"I'm trying to get us out of here."

"You shouldn't do that," said Bogdan. "We have to wait till the adults open it from the outside."

Sage keyed in a number and spoke into the voice activator. "Open hatch." Nothing happened.

"It won't open unless there are two different voice commands." Bogdan was shaking his head furiously.

"Come on, Juliana. You know something must be wrong." Sage looked at her pleadingly.

Juliana went over to the hatch and spoke into the voice activator. "Open hatch." Nothing happened.

12

"The power's down," said Bogdan. "The lights are still on because of the emergency power system."

"Then we're locked in." There was a touch of panic in Juliana's voice.

"No, everything reverts to manual," said Bogdan.

That was just like Bogdan. He had known that for hours. Juliana should have known that, too. Why did she always panic when confronted by technology? Most kids were completely comfortable with technology. But thanks to her father, technology was a mystery to Juliana. She always assumed it was complicated, even when it wasn't. Sage pulled up the hatch. It slid half-way up, then stopped. Sage poked his head out.

"You might want to take this." Bogdan handed Juliana a small radiation detector unit. She took one look at its flashing readout and gave it to Sage. He went out into the hall.

"It's okay. The radiation's still high, but it's at an acceptable level." Juliana ducked through the opening.

> **revert**: To return to a former condition.

They'd gone through disaster drills every month with only the emergency power system. But this time it was for real. The halls were dimly lit with orange lights. Shutters had automatically closed over all the windows because of the radiation level.

Providus wasn't a big space station. With only eight people, it didn't need to be. It was circular, like a big doughnut. The central passage was a ring. The control rooms, laboratories, and workshops were on the outer edge, facing out into the universe. The recreation rooms and sleeping quarters were on the inside.

Juliana's father had chosen the ship's name. All International Space Authority spaceships had Latin names so that different countries couldn't argue about which language should be used. *Providus* meant "thinking ahead to the future."

Sage found his stepmother first. She was lying in the hallway outside the control room. His father was in the control room, slumped over the relocation controls. They were both in full radiation suits. It didn't seem to have helped.

Latin: A language used for scientific terms.

Juliana knew where her own father would be—

in the room where he kept his precious plants. She ran around the hallway. Her father was lying in a tangle of shield foil. He had been trying to protect the plants from radiation. He had fallen across a tray of tiny wheat plants. That had shocked Juliana most. When she saw the precious plants from Earth squashed and broken, she knew something terrible had happened.

The other children were still in the control room in various stages of shock. Bogdan was looking at the ceiling, not wanting to believe what had happened. Diona was screaming, "They're dead. They're all dead. We're all going to die!"

Juliana's legs were giving way. It was as if her bones had turned to ice cream and were starting to melt. She stumbled into a chair. Sage seemed to come out of his trance. He went over to look at his father. He pulled off the helmet of the radiation suit and touched his father's face. He felt the pulse on his neck.

"He's not dead," said Sage.

Juliana snapped out of her panic and went back to her own father's body. Sure enough, his skin was still warm. She could still feel his pulse.

The kids got the adults to the medical clinic and hooked them up to the Vitastat. The Vitastat ran tests

that told them what was wrong with their parents. They found out that the radiation suits, which were supposed to protect the adults, had received the wrong information from the ship's computers. The suits had injected the adults with a mixture of nutrients that put them into a coma. The machine was supposed to suggest treatment, but it didn't seem to know what to do.

They all looked at their sleeping parents. What should they do? Any other time, the adults would have made all the decisions. The children would have done what they were told. Now they had to figure out what to do by themselves.

"The computer system's dead. So is the power grid," Diona sobbed. "We're going to die."

"The emergency power will keep going forever. No one's going to die. We won't run out of food. There's plenty of food," said Sage. "Anyway, we'll be rescued before then. Someone get the disaster manual."

Sage took over. He gave everyone a job to do: checking food stocks, testing the water supply to make sure it was clean, transferring the adults to life-support cocoons, checking the air for radiation and carbon dioxide levels.

"The radiation has wiped out the electronics. The transceiver is destroyed," Bogdan said in his annoying matter-of-fact voice. "It can't be repaired." He made it sound as if it was no more important than if they'd run out of chocolate ice cream. Maybe all New Euros spoke like that.

Juliana watched the others as they took in this information. Sage thumbed through the disaster manual. Diona whimpered like a lost dog. Bogdan stared at the blank computer screens. Juliana wanted to do something, but she couldn't think of anything.

"Do you think it's safe to open the shields?" Juliana was sure that she'd be able to think more clearly if she could see the familiar green and blue of the planet Narelle.

"Solar flares in this system usually decay after three hours. This one was . . ." Bogdan's stream of information was interrupted when they were all thrown to the floor by a sudden movement. The space station was supposed to be in a geostationary orbit around Narelle. They were flung against a wall as the station lurched in another direction.

"What's happening? Why is *Providus* moving?"

> **geostationary orbit**: When a satellite stays above the same spot on a planet's surface as the planet rotates.

Not even Bogdan had a theory for that. Sage looked at the radiation gauge. "Radiation levels are rising. Juliana, you go and shield the adults. I'll get the others strapped down in the shield room."

Juliana ran to the medical clinic. She stood over the life-support cocoon that held the peaceful sleeping body of her father. She looked at all the buttons on the control panel and started to sweat. Why did her father have to be such a mintech? Why did he insist she have a Chandana education? It was the only thing they ever argued about.

Mintechs valued technology. But they thought it was dangerous to be totally reliant on it. The Chandana theory taught children to live without technology as much as possible. They weren't allowed to use technological tools until they turned fifteen. They could access databases for educational purposes, but they couldn't use computers, calculators, or even kitchen gadgets. There were no electronic toys and no holographic games—games that projected three-dimensional images. The only videos they could watch were educational ones. It made Juliana feel stupid.

"You can do this," she told herself. She started to say the alphabet backward. That always calmed her. "Technology is made for technodummies, people who can't think," she reminded herself.

It wasn't that hard. A button on the control panel had "RADIATION SHIELD" printed next to it. Juliana pressed it. A metal cover slid over the cocoon. She quickly did the same for the other two cocoons and then ran back to the shield room.

The others were all strapped down into impact seats. The space station pitched again. Diona squealed. The voice-activated toy on the floor started playing "Twinkle, Twinkle Little Star." Sage looked around.

"Where's Astrid? She's not in the shield room. You were supposed to look after her, Diona."

Diona didn't move. Sage undid his harness and ran out of the shield room. Juliana followed him. They found Astrid playing on the floor in the main control room. Sage scooped her up.

Just then the emergency power system decided that they could do without gravity. Their feet left the floor. They floated out into the hallway until another jolt sent them on a collision course with the walls. They made their way back to the shield room by kicking off the walls at an angle. Astrid

thought it was great fun and squealed with laughter.

Sage was smiling, too, until *Providus* jolted again and he crashed into a fire extinguisher. He lost his grip on Astrid. The child slowly cartwheeled toward the opposite wall. There was a sculpture mounted on that wall. It represented bonds between all nations on Earth. It had sharp metallic spikes with stiff plastic flags. If Astrid hit it, she could get really hurt.

Sage looked confused. He seemed to have forgotten about Astrid. Juliana was starting to feel dizzy. She pushed off from the wall and made a grab for the child. She caught hold of Astrid's arm just before the toddler crashed into the sculpture. Astrid started to cry. She had never liked Juliana.

"Sage, the oxygen's been reduced. We have to get to the shield room."

Sage clumsily grabbed at whatever he could get his hands on. He dragged himself toward the door of the shield room. Juliana had more control. She pushed herself off the walls and aimed herself and Astrid through the shield room hatch. Juliana slammed the hatch down with one hand. Then she strapped Astrid in and helped Sage's fumbling fingers do up his restraint harness. None of this was easy. She was still floating around the room.

Gravity returned suddenly. Juliana bashed her ribs on the arm of Sage's chair as she dropped heavily to the floor. She crawled toward one of the free seats as the *Providus* started to pitch and move. Finally, the ship was stable long enough for her to claw her way into the seat and do up the restraint harness.

That was the last they knew of stability for the next few hours. No one could see what was happening to the space station. From the way they were moving, Juliana imagined the craft was being tossed around like one of Astrid's toys.

It seemed as if the ship would be shaken to pieces. She opened her eyes. The walls of the shield room were warped and bulging, as if *Providus* was trying to turn itself inside out. Juliana felt herself rushing away from everything else in the room.

21

Chapter 2
Big Plum

W<small>HEN</small> J<small>ULIANA</small> <small>REGAINED</small> <small>CONSCIOUSNESS</small>, it was pitch dark. She couldn't see a thing. Maybe she was floating in space. Maybe she'd turned into a star, a tiny twinkling speck in the sky—but she didn't think that stars could feel sore all over. She could also hear someone singing. She was pretty sure that if she were out in space, she wouldn't hear singing.

"Up above our ship so high. Like two diamonds in the sky."

It was the song that Astrid's toy had played. The song stopped. Astrid started to whimper.

"It's okay, Astrid," Sage said. "Just another couple of minutes and it won't be dark anymore."

He started singing the song again. Before he had finished, the lights came on and revealed Sage standing by the control panel. The lights were dim.

"Everybody okay?" he asked.

There were enough groans and grunts to convince Sage that everyone was still alive.

Juliana undid her harness and slid out of the impact seat. Her feet took a little longer than usual to reach the floor. She had time to feel her sore ribs. She thought that one might be broken.

"What's wrong, Sage? Why is the gravity low."

"Everything's low. We lost part of the emergency power grid in the last flare. It's conserving power."

Juliana tried to figure out what all this meant. Her brain still wasn't working very fast. Probably because the oxygen was being conserved, too.

Sage was busy handing out food and drinks to everyone. Juliana had known Sage ever since she could remember. She had always thought of him as a games freak, a technodummy. He handed her a foil pack and drink bottle. Now, Juliana had to admit, he was handling things well. He was calm, thinking clearly, and his technological knowledge was vital.

Juliana was the dummy. Anger against her father surged through her. His antitechnology beliefs meant that in their current situation, Juliana was not much more useful than Astrid.

"Let's get out of this box," said Sage, picking up Astrid and opening the hatch. They followed him down the hall to the recreation room.

Even in the dim light, the bright colors of the posters and kids' drawings cheered everybody up. They all consumed their food and drinks. It had been a while since they'd eaten.

"I've been thinking about what we should do next. I think we should go down to Narelle and wait there until we are rescued," said Sage.

Juliana was a little annoyed that he hadn't asked for her opinion. But at the same time, she was relieved that she didn't have to think about it.

"Why can't we stay here?" asked Diona.

"*Providus*'s emergency power grid was damaged by the last flare. I don't think it has enough power to keep everything going."

The station on the surface of Narelle was incomplete. The facilities there were still pretty basic.

No one liked the idea of leaving the comfort of *Providus*. Sage looked around at them. Juliana had a feeling he was about to tell them something they didn't want to hear.

"It's going to be a while before a rescue team gets here from Earth."

"4.35 years," said Bogdan helpfully. "That's 1,588.881 Earth days, 886.817 Narellean days."

Juliana's insides did a somersault. She had stupidly been thinking that they would be rescued any minute. Diona started to cry. "There must be someone around here who can save us," she blubbered.

Sage shook his head. "Not very likely. No one's been interested in Alpha Centauri since the end of the mining boom fifty years ago."

"There are several abandoned stations on Alpha Centauri's other planets that would have better facilities than the temporary base on Narelle." Bogdan was talking to his food. He never looked at anybody when he spoke.

Sage sighed. "Maybe so, but how would we get there? I wouldn't know how to fly this thing, even if it were fully functional."

Bogdan shrugged his shoulders. He just provided information. Solving problems wasn't his area.

"So, Sage, how do you plan on getting down to Narelle?" asked Juliana.

"Dad let me pilot the Scooter a few times.

I'm pretty sure I could get it down safely."

"Pretty sure?" asked Juliana. The Scooter was the shuttle ship they used to get to the planet's surface.

"The power grid down there should be working. It's permanently shielded. And there are enough supplies. It's the best place to wait it out."

"We can't survive by ourselves for four years. And what about the adults?" asked Juliana.

"We'll keep them in cocoons on Narelle. They'll need a dependable power supply. We can't rely on the power on *Providus* to keep them alive. It's too shaky."

"Okay," said Juliana. She could see that Sage's plan made perfect sense. "You're right." Juliana wanted to do something. "Can we open the shield screens yet?" She gestured toward the radiation meter on Sage's lap.

Sage looked surprised. He'd been expecting her to argue. He didn't bother to thank her, though. "This detector only measures the radiation inside the station," he said. "We'll have to check the exterior scan in the control room."

shuttle: *A vehicle that travels back and forth on short trips.*

They all followed Sage to the control room. They watched

as Sage rerouted some of the precious power to the external scanner.

"It's okay. The last flare was just on Alpha Centauri B. It only lasted a few minutes. Outside radiation levels are safe. We can open the shields."

Diona stopped blubbering and smiled. Even Bogdan looked pleased. The thought of seeing the friendly green and blue planet and the familiar two suns gave them hope.

Juliana couldn't remember what day it was. She checked her watch—18:30, day 53. They would be able to see both suns. The yellow sun of Alpha Centauri A would be above Narelle. The orange sun of Alpha Centauri B would be disappearing behind her.

It would be good to see the suns, even though the suns were the cause of all their problems. She envied Sage his technical knowledge. He could do all kinds of things without thinking—operating equipment, rerouting power, making the suns appear. She would never have been able to do these things. Without Sage, they probably would have died.

Sage rerouted the power again to open the shields. The shutters all zapped back at the same time, revealing the universe. The smiles disappeared from all their faces as they stared at the view through the

ports. Sage opened his mouth, but no words came out.

They weren't looking at the bright green and blue surface of the planet Narelle, which they'd been circling for the past five years. The planet outside their port windows was much bigger than Narelle and looked nothing like it. *Providus* was orbiting the wrong planet. This one was dark purple with dirty white rings around it. It didn't look friendly at all.

"That's Da Li," said Bogdan.

For once, the others didn't need his information. They had only seen pictures of this planet in books before. Still, they could all recognize Da Li, one of the other planets in the Alpha Centauri system. Chinese astronomers had originally discovered it and named it. Its name meant Big Plum. An International Space Authority (ISA) probe later found evidence of valuable mineral deposits on Da Li and on Hong Tao, another of Alpha Centauri's planets.

The ISA didn't have a lot of money to spend on space exploration, even though sixty governments funded it. Countries had more important things to spend their money on. All the ISA could afford was unmanned probes. When private companies heard about the mineral wealth on Da Li and Hong Tao, they started to take an interest in space travel.

Within ten years, they had developed near-light-speed spaceships. Hundreds of companies had set up mining stations on the distant planets. It took them only twenty-five years to strip both planets of their minerals. The mineral dust now permanently blown around by howling winds gave Da Li the appearance of being surrounded by dirty white rings. The dust was all that was left of the once rich mineral supplies.

They'd be able to see the other formerly mineral-rich planet, Hong Tao, or Red Peach, when both suns went behind Narelle.

"How did we get here?"

"We've been flung out of Narelle's orbit and into orbit around Da Li," said Sage. "It must have been the solar flares."

"That's impossible," said Bogdan. As usual, he showed no emotion. Based on his reaction, they could have been talking about a ball rolling off a table.

probe (space probe): A spacecraft that records information about celestial bodies.

29

"It is possible, because we're here," said Diona.

Sage looked out at the dark planet as if he were trying to will it to be Narelle. His father had discovered the friendly planet and had named it after his mother.

"Can we go down to the surface of Da Li and stay there?" asked Juliana.

"I'm sure it would be okay," said Diona hopefully. "Miners lived there for years."

"I don't know if I can get all the equipment functioning again," said Sage. "And we can't breathe the atmosphere. It's too risky."

"The winds would probably tear the Scooter to pieces," added Bogdan.

Juliana tried to imagine four years in an underground building, too scared to go outside for fear of being ripped apart by fierce winds. No one had even mentioned the sulfuric acid in the air that slowly ate through breathing equipment.

"Can't we go back to Narelle?"

"We haven't got enough fuel."

The plan that they had all been complaining about five minutes ago was suddenly appealing. Juliana would have given anything to be on Narelle now. It had oxygen and a good climate. It was waterlogged,

but they could have lived there. They could have grown food. Da Li was a different story.

"But we have to . . ."

"Everyone shut up," said Sage, losing his cool. "I've got to think. I've got to figure out what to do."

Bogdan was staring out of the port. He looked comfortable now that he had something that looked like a screen to stare at.

"There's something out there," he said.

"Yeah, the universe," said Juliana.

Juliana followed the direction of Bogdan's gaze. A small dot was emerging from Da Li's purple haze. It disappeared for a moment among the planet's rings and then was visible again, bigger.

"It's a spacecraft," said Diona. "We're saved!"

Chapter 3

Message from Home

Fact: The NASA Deep Space Network is an international network of three radio telescopes. The telescopes explore space and keep track of spacecraft as Earth rotates.

S AGE STARTED flicking switches, and the lights inside the Providus went out.

"What are you doing?" asked Juliana. "They won't see us if the ship's in darkness."

"That's the general idea," said Sage.

"Have you gone crazy?" Juliana asked him.

"Space pirates," said Bogdan.

"They must be space pirates," agreed Sage. "Who else would be a trillion miles from anywhere? The minerals are all mined out. The only reason anybody would be going down to Da Li would be to salvage the equipment."

"But that's illegal."

"Yes, Diona. That's why they're called pirates. There's no reason they would be interested in us," Sage explained. "We just have to play dead."

"Are you sure they wouldn't help us?"

"Illegal space salvage is a serious crime. They're not going to risk a death sentence for a few kids."

"Don't you remember we learned about pirates murdering people on distant stations during the mining boom?" Bogdan paid more attention in class than anyone else.

"They let other people do all the work. Then they killed them and stole the minerals," said Juliana.

"They're heading this way." There was a note of panic in Diona's voice.

"I've turned off everything I can. The ship is pretty beaten up. Hopefully, they'll think it's inactive."

"But they might try to salvage *Providus*."

"I doubt it. It's not worth much to them. They're looking for mining equipment and the latest small craft to sell on the black market."

black market: A group of people who buy and sell things illegally.

The spacecraft was closer now. They could make out its shape. Suddenly, a bright beam of light shone out in their direction from the craft. Sage pushed them down to the floor. "Stay down. It's a searchlight. They're looking for survivors."

Juliana nearly jumped out of her skin when a voice boomed over the speaker on the control panel.

"This is the All-nations recovery ship *Albatross*. Please indicate if there are crew members aboard. We are able to offer help, should you require it."

Diona opened her mouth. Sage clapped his hand over her mouth to stop her from speaking. With his other hand, he turned off their own loudspeaker.

"Again. If you need help, our mother ship is equipped with a transceiver for communication with any Earth nation." The same message was repeated in Chinese, French, and Arabic.

The ship passed them and began to get smaller.

"It's okay, they're not interested."

"But they said they were a recovery ship," Diona said as soon as Sage took his hand off her mouth.

"They were lying," said Bogdan. "Recovery ships have to display the All-nations logo and identify themselves with a special code. They were pirates."

Juliana watched the craft until it disappeared.

"That's the closest we'll get to other humans for the next four years or more." She had a stupid urge to shout "Wait, don't leave us!" It had been nine-and-a-half years since they had left Earth. In that time they hadn't seen a single human being other than the members of their own small group. Why did she suddenly feel a need for contact with other people?

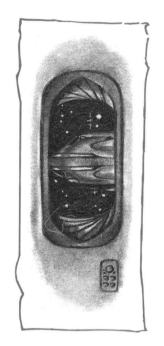

"Maybe the pirates aren't so bad," said Diona.

"Yeah, maybe they're just misunderstood."

Everyone was worn out. Even though they had lost consciousness during their unexpected flight to Da Li, they were all tired. They all recognized the effects of low oxygen. They had experienced it on Narelle.

"Diona, help me get Astrid to sleep," said Sage. "She needs to feel like everything's normal."

Sure, thought Juliana. Her parents are cocooned like caterpillars. We're parked next to the wrong planet. And there's no one but a bunch of pirates for a trillion miles. That's normal.

Bogdan was fiddling with the communications panel.

"What are you doing? You're not sending a message to the pirates, are you?"

"No. There's a message in the communications log."

"I thought we couldn't communicate with anybody."

"We can't. The transceiver was wrecked during the second set of flares."

Having a conversation with Bogdan was difficult. He never volunteered any information. He only answered direct questions.

"So, what are you doing exactly?"

"There's a stored message in the log."

Juliana was losing her patience. "You already said that. What does it mean, Bogdan?"

"It must have been received before the transceiver burned out. The data has to be reassembled. Instantaneous messages arrive scrambled."

"Can you reassemble it?"

"Of course. But it will take time."

Juliana wasn't sure how it all worked, but she knew the theory of instantaneous communication.

Wormholes in space had been discovered just before they left Earth. They were just like scientists and science-fiction writers had predicted: holes in the time–space continuum that linked points that were many light-years apart. It turned out that *wormholes* was a very appropriate name.

Unlike the wormholes in fiction, which could transport space vehicles, the real wormholes were very narrow. Not much wider than a worm. The only things that could travel down them were electronic signals. There was so much turbulence in a wormhole that the information from the signals was all mixed up when it arrived. Each bit of information had to have a marker so that they all could be pieced together when the message got to the other end.

Juliana felt useless. She was no good with children and no good with technology, either.

By the time Sage and Diona got back to the control room, Bogdan had reassembled the message.

"It's not specifically for the *Providus*. It's just an Earth news bulletin, sent to all outposts. There should be pictures, too, but I've only unscrambled the audio."

time-space continuum: *The idea that time and space are continuous—one can flow into the other.*

"Let's hear it."

The first item was about fighting that had broken out between New Euro and the United African States (UAS) over a tiny piece of land. World leaders talked about the possibility of global war. There were other items about international trade. There was a silly piece about the latest trend in Japanese pets—a cross between a dog and a cat.

Diona was trying to pick an argument with Bogdan.

"New Euros are all stupid," she was saying. "The UAS will lick them in two seconds flat."

Diona was always trying to argue with Bogdan about the superiority of UAS versus New Europe.

"Diona," replied Bogdan calmly, "People call me lots of names, but stupid isn't one I ever hear."

"Shush, you two," said Sage sharply. "Listen. There is one more piece of news."

"The International Space Administration announced today that it would not send a search party to Alpha Centauri after the recent solar flares. A spokesperson said that images from the planet Narelle showed the space station *Providus* had been destroyed. There has been no communication from the scientists. The ISA has concluded that there were no survivors. The loss of all on board is a tragedy."

There was complete silence for a few minutes as they tried to figure out what the message meant.

"*Providus* isn't destroyed. They made a mistake."

"It's not a mistake, Diona," said Sage. "It's a lie."

"You mean no one's coming for us?" She asked.

"It would cost billions of dollars to rescue us. Why should they waste all that money on a few people?"

Juliana looked at Sage, hoping that he might be working out a plan. His face was pale. He looked back at Juliana. The look was blank, without hope. It scared her.

No one said anything else. They all went to their own sleeping quarters. Funny, thought Juliana. Before, they wanted each other's company. Now, they wanted to be alone.

More than twelve hours had passed when Juliana awoke. She couldn't believe she had slept so long. She got up and walked around *Providus*. The others were still asleep. The silence was strange. Not that it ever used to be noisy. But there was always somebody around and always some machinery beeping or humming. There was something else missing, too. Before, music was always playing. Juliana walked around the ring three times. It helped to wake her up.

Juliana knocked on Sage's door. There was no

response. She knocked again. After a few minutes, the door opened and Sage's sleep-creased face appeared.

"What?"

"I thought we should talk about what to do."

"There's nothing to do."

"Sage, we can't just lie down and die," said Juliana angrily. "There must be something we can do."

Sage shut the door in her face. Juliana was furious with him. She had learned to trust Sage, to rely on him to come up with the answers to their problems. Now he had given up. Juliana tried to wake up Diona and Bogdan, but she couldn't.

She went to visit her father. She looked down at his peaceful, sleeping face. There he was, as close as he had always been, but he might as well have been on the other side of the universe. He was always good at solving problems that involved his plants. But she had no idea what he might do in a situation like this.

Juliana had read the disaster manual from cover to

cover. Unfortunately, there wasn't a chapter entitled *What to Do If You're Stranded Four Light-years from Earth and Your Parents Are in Comas.*

There was no one to help her. Was it going to be up to her to save them? What did she know? She could grow a healthy plant from a broken twig. She could make a meal without using a single processed product. She could even weave fabric using natural fibers.

Juliana's father had thought that if there was a disaster, they would all have been stranded on Narelle. He had taught her the survival skills that he thought she would need in such a situation. The skills she really needed, he had forbidden her to learn.

Chapter 4

Strawberries and Miso Soup

Fact: Once a spacecraft is moving in space, there is no gravity or friction to slow it down. It will keep moving at the same speed. This is called continuous motion.

JULIANA COULDN'T accept it. She couldn't imagine spending the rest of her life on *Providus*, with no contact with Earth. Even though she had lived on the station for more than nine years, there was always the promise of a life on Narelle.

Narelle was a wild planet where giant plants grew as you watched them, where it rained almost nonstop. If you weren't careful, you could be sitting on a hill one minute, and find yourself thirty feet underwater the next. The adults had planned a base on Narelle where they could all watch the natural wonders of the planet through huge, flood-proof windows.

Juliana liked Narelle. That's where she had imagined spending the rest of her life. Other people would have joined them once the base was operational. It wasn't meant to be a colony. But Juliana's father was convinced that others would want to get away from crowded Earth and its angry, aggressive people.

The other kids on *Providus* had always made fun of Juliana because of her nontechnological education. They often fought amongst themselves, but they could suddenly gang up on her if she ever wanted to do anything her way. She had never been best friends with any of them. Her father had been her best friend. Now, the other kids were all she had.

What could she do? The only thing she had was her Chandana teachings. The Chandana system stressed how to assess resources and plan a strategy. Basically, that meant how to make the best of a bad situation. It was something that Juliana was good at. Now, she just had to put her theories into action.

Before she woke the others, Juliana made a meal. She didn't simply prepare dried vegetables from a packet. Instead, she made a meal from scratch and served it on plates. She used fresh vegetables grown by her father as part of an experiment to test their growth rate with different fertilizers.

The time for experiments was over. She waited

until the others had finished eating the rice and vegetables and then brought out a bowl of strawberries. Astrid was delighted. Her cheerfulness didn't spread.

"We have to decide what to do," said Juliana when they had all finished. "We can't give up. We need to start by making a list of our resources."

"This is some Chandana mumbo jumbo, isn't it?" said Sage.

"Come on, Sage," said Juliana. "I did everything you asked me to do before. You may have given up, but I haven't. You could give my ideas a try."

"I'm not doing it."

Juliana ignored him and spread a large piece of paper on the floor. "One thing we have is *Providus*," she said. She wrote "Space Station" at the top of the paper. "Now we have to search *Providus* and make a list of everything that might be useful." No one moved.

"Diona and I will make a list of the food items. Sage and Bogdan, you can find out if there's any equipment that's still working."

"I'm not doing it," said Sage. "It's a waste of time."

Juliana managed to get Diona and Bogdan moving. She gave up on Sage.

Diona wasn't good at making lists. For one thing, she couldn't write. "I could do it if I had a keyboard," she said cheerfully.

"Never mind," said Juliana. "You tell me what's in the boxes. I'll make the list."

Juliana was rather proud of her writing. It was one of the few things about her education that she liked. The other kids learned keyboard skills, but they didn't use them much. Most of the time they input information verbally. It always seemed like cheating to Juliana. Anyway, putting words together letter by letter and sentences word by word had always been a pleasure. She wrote her list in her neatest handwriting with lots of loops, just to show Diona what she was missing.

"Why is there so much miso soup? There's tons."

"Don't exaggerate," said Juliana. Miso soup was her father's favorite. He had brought enough to last for years.

When they met back in the recreation room, Sage hadn't moved. But he had written

miso: A high-protein food of soybeans, salt, and grains.

45

"completely nonfunctional" after "Space Station" on Juliana's list. Astrid had made some drawings on the paper, including one of a wobbly spaceship next to the writing. Bogdan had a list, too—a string of abbreviations and symbols that Juliana couldn't read.

"You'd better read it to me," said Juliana.

"First, there is the emergency power system," announced Bogdan. "The water recycling system, the minimal atmosphere, and the gravity maintainer."

"Yeah, we knew about that already," said Diona. "We can breathe and we're not floating."

Juliana started adding these items to the list.

"Let him finish, Diona. Sometimes we forget the obvious. Go on, Bogdan."

"The equipment in the plant room works." That didn't surprise Juliana. Her father always made sure his plants weren't dependent on computers.

"Anything else?"

"Yes. Two laser disc players, four wristpads, one hair-curling device, one foot massager, and one facial-hair shaver."

"Great," said Sage. "In about five years, you'll be able to shave. Until then you'll just have to be satisfied with curly hair and relaxed feet."

Juliana wrote all the items down. "They all have parts that could be useful," she said.

"What's on your list?" asked Bogdan.

"There's a lot of food. It's freeze-dried so we'll have no problem keeping it. It's enough to last for years."

"But not forever," pointed out Bogdan.

"We've got no computers, no communications, no parents," said Diona. "And we can't do anything without them. We have no future." Tears rolled down her face again. This wasn't how it worked in class.

"We still have all the facilities on Narelle," Juliana said, trying to sound positive.

"Unfortunately, Narelle is five million miles away."

"How much fuel do we have?"

"Hardly any," said Bogdan sulkily. "The fuel's all in tanks on Narelle."

"Even if we had fuel, *Providus* is in no shape to make the trip," said Sage. "Without computers it won't move. You're just getting everybody's hopes up. It's pointless and cruel."

Juliana sat down, stung by Sage's words. She hated to admit it, but she was just about ready to give up.

"We got here without fuel," said Diona.

Juliana looked at Diona in surprise. "That's right,

we did." Diona was the last person she had expected to contribute anything useful. "How did we do that?"

"The solar flares must have created a force that set *Providus* in motion and pushed it out of its orbit," said Sage.

"Impossible." Bogdan was shaking his head. "Solar flares don't do that."

Sage ignored him and continued.

"Once out of Narelle's atmosphere, there was no gravity to stop it. It just kept moving at the same speed until it was drawn into Da Li's orbit."

"So if we could get something to give *Providus* a push in the right direction, we could get to Narelle?"

"Sure. If we could get it moving," said Bogdan. "Which we can't."

In class these exercises always worked. In class there was always just Juliana and her father. He always thought positively. He always came up with something. Her eyes started to fill with tears. Not tears of sadness, but tears of anger. Anger at all of these technodummies. Especially Sage. He wouldn't even try. Maybe she had to admit it. In real life, the Chandana theories were useless.

Astrid was squashing a strawberry onto the white paper. Juliana looked at the child's drawing.

"That's not *Providus*," she snapped. "You drew the wrong spaceship."

Sage jumped to his sister's defense. "She's never been outside of *Providus*. How's she supposed to know what it looks like? That's the Scooter she's drawn. Can't you see that? She likes to watch the Scooter take off. Well, she used to."

Juliana saw a ray of hope. "Did anyone check to see if the Scooter was working?"

"Its computers would all have blown, just like on *Providus*."

Juliana was deflated. "So we can't use it."

"The Scooter has manual override controls." It was the first positive thing Sage had said. "Everyone knew that with two suns there was twice as much chance of solar flares. The Scooter had to be able to function if there was a flare while it was in flight."

"Does the Scooter have enough fuel to take us to Narelle?"

"Nowhere near," answered Sage.

"Enough to get us out of Da Li's atmosphere?"

manual override: Taken over by a system worked by hand, not by machine.

"Yes, easily."

"And you know how to pilot it, Sage?"

Sage nodded. There was a silence. A different sort of silence from the sullen, miserable silence of before. This was a silence where people were thinking. Juliana added things to her list: *Scooter, Fuel, Pilot*.

"So if we can get the Scooter out of Da Li's atmosphere and point it in the direction of Narelle, then it should just keep going. Is that right?"

"Yes . . . in theory."

"Then all we have to do is land it."

"I've never actually landed the Scooter," said Sage. "But I know how to do it . . . in theory."

Just for a moment, everyone had livened up. Just for a moment, they had had a glimpse of renewed hope. It didn't last long.

"So this is your plan, Juliana. We go careening off into space in the approximate direction of Narelle. If we get there, we then hope that Sage can do a crash course . . ." Juliana winced at Diona's choice of words ". . . in landing a Series 6 Shuttle Craft. If we land in one piece, we hope it's somewhere near the base. If we find the base, we hope that it hasn't been wrecked by the solar flares. Is that

careening: *Speeding wildly from side to side.*

what you're saying?"

Diona could be annoyingly realistic sometimes.

"Look, I didn't say it was the perfect plan," said Juliana defensively.

"Are you sure the Scooter is in working condition?" asked Diona.

They all waited in the control room while Sage checked the Scooter. The control room had the biggest windows and the best view of the universe. Looking out from the control room, there was no escaping the truth. The *Providus* was a tiny dot in the universe. Around them was endless space speckled with millions of stars. Each was another sun. One of those specks was Sol, the sun that shone on Earth.

Sage returned. "I checked all of the Scooter's communications and computer equipment," he said. "It's not working."

"Did you check the manual controls?"

"Yeah. It all works okay."

This was good. Finally they had something positive. A ship that worked. Juliana let the idea sink in.

"We're on our own," she said.

She wasn't trying to be dramatic, she just wanted to state the facts. "No one's coming to get us. The adults' condition hasn't changed. They aren't going to suddenly wake up. There's just us."

"We know that," said Diona. "Why repeat it?"

"We have to decide what we are going to do."

None of the others wanted to take responsibility. Juliana understood. Part of her wanted to go to sleep and not have to worry about it. They weren't used to making life-or-death decisions.

"You're not going to make more lists, are you?" asked Diona.

"We don't need a list. There are only two options. We either stay on *Providus* and wait—until we run out of food or until something critical breaks down," Juliana paused. "Or we take a chance and fly the Scooter back to Narelle."

"Don't tell me, let me guess," said Sage sarcastically. "We have to vote on it."

Juliana nodded. "Who wants to stay on *Providus*?"

Diona and Bogdan put up their hands.

"Who votes to take the Scooter back to Narelle?"

Juliana put up her hand, even though she knew it was a waste of time.

"We win," said Diona.

"I haven't voted yet," said Sage. "I vote we go back to Narelle."

Juliana looked at Sage in disbelief. After going against her all the way, he had voted with her.

"That's two each," said Bogdan.

"Astrid," said Juliana. "Would you like to go with Sage for a ride on the Scooter, or would you like to stay here with Diona?"

"Go with Sage," said Astrid.

Sage smiled. It was the first time Juliana had seen him smile since before the flares.

"That's not fair," said Diona.

"It's fair," said Sage. "You should have played with her occasionally."

I t took them less than two days to get ready for the trip. The Scooter was small compared to *Providus*. It was not much bigger than a small airplane. It was built to carry about twelve passengers. But there were no living quarters. Whoever had designed it hadn't expected it to be going on trips of any more than a few hours. They packed as much food and water as they

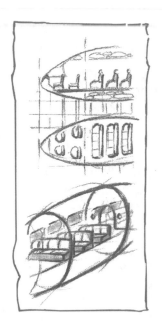

could fit into the Scooter's small hold.

Sage checked and double-checked the spaceship's manual systems. The worst part was putting their parents, in their cocoons, on board the smaller ship. They were risking their parents' lives—and their own. Astrid cried for her mommy for the first time since the flares.

There were two seating areas in the Scooter: up front where the passengers were strapped into impact seats for take-off and landing, and more comfortable seats in a lounge area. They would have to sleep in sleeping bags on the floor. Juliana had set their departure time for 8:00 the following morning. She thought they should have a decent night's sleep before they blasted off into the unknown.

Juliana had expected Diona to take a lot of useless stuff. Sure enough, she showed up with three bags of clothes and toiletries. Juliana was surprised, though, when Bogdan arrived with a large space case. It was crammed full of electronic parts, broken pieces of equipment, and the few working items he had found.

Juliana didn't argue. She had wanted to take a lot of things herself. In the end, she settled on her favorite book, *The Little Prince*, three rocks, and one small but beautiful Narellean plant. Astrid had an armful of soft toys and a worn blanket. Sage had a small bag, which couldn't have held much more than his underwear.

Launching the Scooter was quite simple. Sage pressed some buttons, released the locking clamps, and ignited the booster rockets. The little spaceship shot forward out of the launch bay and into space. It was all over in ten minutes. They had left *Providus* behind.

Chapter 5
Backtracking

Fact: Asteroids are metallic, rocky bodies. Though they orbit the sun, they are too small to be called planets. Asteroids can be as small as a pebble to six hundred miles in diameter.

DA LI LOOKED BIGGER and more threatening away from the safety of *Providus*. The Scooter felt so small and so flimsy alongside the giant planet.

"That was the easy part," said Sage. "Now we have to break free of Da Li's gravitational pull." Sage gently pushed the accelerator.

Juliana was looking forward to getting away from Da Li. Once they saw Narelle again, she was sure everybody would cheer up.

They could feel that the ship was moving faster by the way they were pushed back in their seats. But Da Li didn't seem to be getting any smaller. Juliana had the uneasy feeling that the purple planet was sucking them into its deadly atmosphere.

"Are you sure you're moving away from Da Li, Sage?" said Diona.

"I'm sure. It's a big planet. Because we're moving away from it relatively slowly, you can't see that it's really getting smaller."

The little ship continued to accelerate, straining against the forces trying to hold it back. It shook and vibrated. The vibration was bone-rattling. It was worse than when the *Providus* was being thrown out of Narelle's orbit. They were being tossed left and right, back and forth.

The straps of their harnesses were stretched to the breaking point. The temperature started rising, too. The metal on the outside of the ship was glowing from the heat of friction. The windows were beginning to buckle from the strain. A piece of equipment broke off from the ship's hull and disintegrated. Juliana couldn't help crying out.

"It's okay," said Sage. "That was the transceiver dish. It didn't work anyway. It won't be much longer."

With one last shuddering lurch, the Scooter broke through Da Li's upper atmosphere. The sickening vibration gradually stopped. Sage waited for a few minutes and then released the accelerator. The little ship seemed to be hanging motionless in the dark sky.

"Why have you stopped?" asked Diona.

"I haven't. I released the accelerator. Now that we're in space we'll keep moving at the same speed."

"But it's so slow."

"Not really. We're traveling at 50,000 mph."

Juliana looked out at the stars. "How do you know which one is Narelle?"

Sage smiled. "You'll see, Jules." Then, suddenly, from behind Da Li's smudgy purple outline, a small but beautiful blue and green crescent emerged.

"It's Narelle!" shouted Diona. Everybody clapped.

"We're about five million miles away. At this speed we should be there in about five days."

"Why did it take us less than a day to get to Da Li, but it's going to take us five days to get back?"

"Da Li was passing at its closest point to Narelle when we got blasted out of orbit. Both planets have moved away from each other since then."

"Da Li has a figure-eight orbit around both suns,"

Bogdan informed them. "It is now starting to move away from Alpha Centauri A to revolve around Alpha Centauri B. It will be another seventy years before it gets this close to Narelle again."

Juliana watched the little thrusters on the side of the ship occasionally give off bursts of gas. That was how Sage was directing the ship. A nudge here, a push there, and they would be right on course for Narelle.

Juliana thought of the greenness of Narelle. She thought of the base there, which had seemed unfinished and a little primitive the last time they visited it. Now it seemed like a real haven. Five days isn't so long, she thought.

It didn't take long for the bickering to start. Sage was cranky from the stress of keeping the Scooter on course. Bogdan kept taking apart equipment and leaving the pieces everywhere. Astrid wouldn't sleep and kept them all awake.

Diona was the worst. She went on and on about what a great nation UAS was. She was always trying to annoy Bogdan by saying how disorganized New Europe was and how New Euros were nothing more than peasants. Most of the time Bogdan didn't bite. Sometimes he would start listing the achievements of New Europe. Once he got started, the data just spewed out. Nothing could stop him.

Juliana went up to the bridge and sat with Sage to get away from the noise. After the vote, Sage had worked hard to get the Scooter ready. He might have resisted the process, but once the decision was made to leave *Providus,* he never wavered. Now he was focused on getting them all safely to Narelle.

"How come Diona is so loyal to UAS?" asked Juliana. "She was a tiny baby when you all left."

"My stepmother always encouraged her to be patriotic."

"My father was proud to be American," said Juliana. "He told me all about the beautiful mountains, the trees and animals and stuff, but he never forced it down my throat."

Sage nodded. "My dad never lived in one place long enough to call any one country home. I don't ever remember him calling himself Japanese. He thought of the whole earth as his home, I guess."

"Do you think we'll ever be able to revive them?"

"Will the facilities on Narelle be damaged? Will we be able to survive? Will the suns collide? There are a lot of questions that I don't have answers for, Jules."

"I guess we have to take things one at a time. First, we must get to Narelle. At least that plan's working."

"Don't say that, it's bad luck," said Sage. "We're only half-way there."

Juliana got into the habit of sitting up on the bridge with Sage. It was good to have someone close to her own age to talk to. For the first time in her life she had started to think about what it would be like to have friends. If she was on Earth, she would be friends with lots of kids her age. She would be in class with them every day and would hang out with them in her free time. It was hard to imagine.

Sage looked worried.

"Everything's going all right, isn't it?" she asked.

"Sort of." It wasn't the answer she wanted to hear.

They had been traveling for four days now. Narelle was hanging in the dark sky in front of them like a giant blue and green ball.

"It looks like it would be hard to miss it even if you wanted to," Juliana said.

"It's not as easy as it seems. Narelle isn't standing still. It's actually moving at something like thirty miles an hour. And it's turning. We can't just plop down anywhere. We have to land at the base. That's on the side that's turned away from us now. A slight error would mean we land a couple of hundred miles from the base. I'm not even sure if the Scooter can handle the re-entry. You saw how knocked around we were when we left Da Li's atmosphere."

"Do you ever wish your father had stayed on Earth?" asked Sage eventually.

"Not before all this happened," said Juliana. "But lately I have. It's only been eight days since the flares, and I'm already sick of having to be responsible."

Sage sighed heavily and nodded. "Yeah, it would be nice to goof off for a while."

Juliana was ready to strangle Diona. She was sick to death of Astrid's noisy toys, and Bogdan had to be the most annoying person in the world. He had spent the whole five days playing with his pile of electronic junk. Whenever he was working on a project, he whistled the same three notes over and over again.

She went up to the bridge to see how things were going. Narelle was now back to its "right" size and position. It filled almost all of the sky visible through the forward windows. Juliana was excited. They would finally be arriving on Narelle. And they would, hopefully, revive the adults.

Juliana was really looking forward to having someone tell her what to do. Sage was busy operating the smallest of the thrusters, nudging the ship first one way, then another way. They wanted to be in the best position for re-entry directly above the base.

"Not much longer now," said Juliana proudly. She had made this happen. If it wasn't for her, they would still be orbiting Da Li with no future. She and Sage made a good team. With her planning and his technological skills, they had saved them all. Someone cleared his throat. It was Bogdan.

"I have something to report," he said.

Juliana and Sage both turned to look at him, the same annoyed look on both their faces.

"I have constructed a simple

63

scanner from some of the nonworking equipment from the *Providus*." He held up something that looked like a tangled pile of cables, circuit boards, and other electronic pieces. At the end of the tangle was a small screen.

"Hey," said Sage. "Isn't that Dad's wristpad? Who said you could use that?"

"Father had some useful programs installed in it. They were the key to making this device work."

"I'm glad you've kept yourself amused," said Sage.

"It isn't for my amusement. I've constructed it so that I could scan the vicinity."

"In case there's anybody wandering around looking for us?" Sage and Juliana exchanged a smile.

"No," said Bogdan, looking as serious as he always did. Juliana couldn't ever remember seeing the kid smile. "I thought it might be useful to check that there was nothing in our path that we might collide with."

"Great. I'm glad you're keeping yourself busy."

install: To set in position and connect for use.

"And have you found anything in our path, Bogdan?" asked Juliana.

"No." He was

staring past them through the port. "There is something I should bring to your attention, though. Something is wrong with Narelle."

"What do you mean?" asked Sage.

Sage and Juliana turned to look at the planet. Sure enough, as it was turning toward them they saw that there was a black mark on the planet's surface. The normally greeny-blue color of Narelle was scarred.

"What is it, Sage?"

Sage shook his head. "I don't know."

They spent the next six hours watching in horror as they got closer to Narelle. As the planet turned, the scar on the surface got bigger and bigger. The atmosphere above the scar was thick and gray.

"What's happened to Narelle?" asked Juliana.

"It's been hit by something—an asteroid I'd say, by the size of that scar."

"That must be what knocked *Providus* out of its orbit," said Bogdan. "I knew it couldn't be the flares."

"The thing is, it's right where the base used to be."

"You must push the left side thrusters so that the ship turns away," said Bogdan.

"I know that." Sage's voice was shaking with emotion. "I am."

"What do you mean?" said Diona. "Are we turning away from Narelle?"

"We can't live down there. The base isn't there anymore. The debris that has been thrown into the atmosphere will block the light from the suns. All the vegetation on that side will die. It will be cold. The other side is covered in water."

"What will we do?"

"I don't know."

There was nothing Juliana could do but watch in horror as Narelle slowly slipped by the windows. Within an hour, Narelle was behind them and they were hurtling away from it into unknown space.

Chapter 6
Freefall

Fact: The light from our sun takes only eight minutes to reach Earth. Light from the Andromeda galaxy takes two million years to reach us. Light travels at 180,000 miles per second. Therefore, we are seeing Andromeda as it was two million years ago.

AN EERIE FEELING FILLED the Scooter. The children knew they were doomed. Diona was quiet. Bogdan just stared out of the rear window at Narelle getting smaller and smaller. Even Astrid seemed to sense that something bad was happening. She was crying and calling out for Sage.

Juliana went up to the bridge where Sage was sitting by himself.

"Astrid is upset."

"I don't want to talk to anyone."

"It's not your fault that Narelle got hit by an asteroid," said Juliana. "If anyone's at fault it's me. If it wasn't for me, we would still be on _Providus_."

Sage didn't answer.

"So you're going to sit and stare into space until we starve to death? It'll take a while, you know. We've got lots of supplies."

"Not that long," said Sage quietly. "There's no recycling unit on the Scooter. We'll run out of water in a few days."

Juliana had never really thought about dying. Suddenly it was looming very close.

"There must be something we can do."

Sage smiled sadly at her. "Get out a big piece of paper, if it makes you feel better."

Juliana didn't need to write it down. It was simple. If they stayed on the Scooter, they would die. If they were to survive, they had to get off the Scooter. The only way they could do that was to land the ship. Juliana had to face it—there were some situations in which no amount of thinking or organizing would change things. They were at the mercy of the universe.

Juliana went back to the lounge area. Diona was curled up in her sleeping bag. Astrid was playing with one of her noisy toys. It was a particularly annoying one. It didn't play a tune. It just made a monotonous beeping noise.

Juliana sighed. She was irritated. "Okay, Astrid, let's find something else to play with." Juliana knelt down to pick up the offending toy.

"That's not one of your toys," she said. "That's Bogdan's device."

There were rows of numbers scrolling across the small screen as the beeping continued.

Juliana took the tangle of electronic pieces to the rear of the ship. Bogdan was still staring out at the shrinking planet.

"If you don't shut this thing up, Bogdan, I'm going to jump on it."

Bogdan turned around and looked at his invention. He took it from Juliana and keyed some commands.

"My device has detected something nearby."

"What sort of something? Another asteroid?"

"It is not a celestial body."

"What do you mean?"

"It isn't a comet or an asteroid. It's a spacecraft."

Juliana grabbed hold of Bogdan fiercely. She could

> **celestial body**: Any of the visible objects in space, such as planets, moons, stars, asteroids, comets.

barely stop herself from shaking the information out of him.

"What sort of spacecraft? A satellite, a probe, a mining drone? What?"

Bogdan was shaking his head. "No, it's big. Very big. It could be a—"

Juliana was already racing up to the bridge. "It doesn't matter what it is," she yelled over her shoulder. "It's our only chance. We have to show Sage."

Sage was still sitting at the control panel as if he was in control of the ship.

"Sage, there's a spacecraft out there."

Sage turned to them with a look that said they had to be joking.

"Show him, Bogdan."

Bogdan pointed to the readout on his strange piece of equipment.

"What does that mean? Can't you get an image?"

"No, it's just data. But it's there all right."

"What are you waiting for, Sage?" said Juliana, infuriated with both of them.

"Okay! What are the coordinates?"

Bogdan keyed in commands. "Here," he pointed to the screen. "Can you understand them?"

"Yes, of course I can," snapped Sage.

"This is no time for fighting." Juliana was almost jumping up and down with impatience. "How far away is it?"

"It's only about twenty thousand miles away. We're still traveling at re-entry speed. That's about forty thousand miles per hour."

"That means we'll be there in half an hour."

"Yeah. If I can put the Scooter on a direct course toward it."

"Can you?"

"There's not much fuel left to operate the thrusters, but I think I can."

Sage used his wristpad to calculate the angle that the Scooter would have to turn to reach the coordinates. He got Bogdan to check them and then pushed the thrusters.

Diona had come up to see what was going on.

She had Astrid on one hip.

Fifteen minutes passed. Twenty, then twenty-five. Still no sign of a spacecraft.

"Shouldn't we be able to see it by now?" asked Juliana.

"Yes." Juliana had hoped for more information.

"It's your stupid machine, Bogdan," said Diona. "It's not working."

Bogdan peered at the readout of his device and tapped on the keyboard.

"We should be right in front of it."

"Well, we're not," said Diona.

"I want to look through the scopes, Sage," said Astrid, wriggling out of Diona's arms and crawling up into her brother's lap.

"Astrid," said Juliana. "This is no time for games."

"Ease off, Jules," said Sage. "What difference does it make? We might as well all go and play games."

Juliana bit her lip. She wanted to do something. She wanted to rush around pressing buttons, making calculations. Sage pulled down the binocular scopes to where Astrid could look through them. He was as calm as she had ever seen him. He was ready to die, Juliana could see that.

"Big spaceship," said Astrid still looking through the scopes but pointing a finger out of the window.

Everybody looked out of the window. There was only the usual view of space: black with specks of light.

Sage looked through the scopes and nearly jumped out of his seat. "It's huge."

He looked from the scopes to the window, to the scopes and back through the window again. Then he climbed up over the console and pulled the polarizing screen down over the windows. "Astrid turned on the polarizer on the scopes. That's why she could see it. Look." An enormous black spaceship materialized in front of them. Juliana couldn't believe her eyes. She had never imagined that a spacecraft could be so huge.

"It's coated in a substance that is not shiny, but it still reflects the sky," said Bogdan. "It acts as a camouflage."

"It must be a hundred times bigger than *Providus*," she gasped.

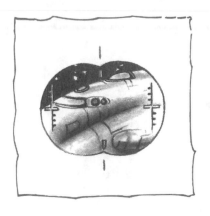

"I told you I'm never wrong," said Bogdan, not at all excited.

"How far away are we? Have they seen us?"

"We're still about a thousand miles away, but you would think they would have picked us up by now."

"There are no markings on the ship," said Bogdan in his usual dispassionate way. "Where is it from?"

The excited buzz suddenly died.

"What exactly is a ship that size doing way out here?"

"If there was any such size ship, we would have known about it."

"Any Earth ship," said Diona ominously.

Juliana looked at Sage and Bogdan. "Surely you don't think it's an alien ship, do you?"

"What other explanation is there? I've never heard of anything this size being built on Earth."

They were getting closer and closer. The spacecraft was getting bigger and bigger.

"There is another possibility, besides its being an alien ship," said Diona. "Can you see those three spaceships tethered to the loading dock?"

"Barely."

Diona had good vision. "Look at the middle one."

They all strained to make out the craft.

"Does it look familiar?"

"Oh, no," said Juliana. "It's that pirate ship that passed us back at Da Li."

They all looked at each other in horror.

"It's a pirate base. That's why it's camouflaged."

"Don't dock with it, Sage," said Diona. "We don't want to have our throats slit."

"We don't have a choice. They've locked onto us. We're being pulled toward it."

Chapter 7

Who's Been Sitting in My . . .

Fact: Originally, pirates were people who robbed ships at sea. The term is now used to mean people who rob aircraft and spacecraft as well.

THERE WAS NOTHING they could do but sit and watch as the giant ship hauled them in—like an ugly spider reeling in a trapped insect. Its dull black presence was terrifying. The invisible force drew them closer and closer. Then they were up against the hull.

A bay door slid back and the little Scooter was sucked inside the ship. Locking clamps reached out and docked it. The bay door closed.

Outside the little ship they could hear the whooshing sound of recompression as air filled the docking berth. Bogdan and Diona were white with fear. Juliana's heart was beating so hard she thought it would burst out of her chest. She waited, expecting burly, ugly pirates to fling the hatch open and mow them down with laser cannons. But nothing happened.

Sage opened the hatch, looked out, and sniffed. The air was fresh and good after the stale, recycled atmosphere of the Scooter.

"We're probably so insignificant, we're not worth worrying about," he said.

What was in store for them? Juliana tried to imagine what pirates would do with a bunch of kids. Make them into slaves? Imprison them? No, why would they bother? There was no way around it— they would most likely kill them.

The children climbed out of the Scooter. Another door slid open. Beyond the opening seemed to be the inside of the pirate spaceship.

"Wow," said Sage, forgetting his fear as he stared in awe. "I've never seen anything like this. Never dreamed of anything like this."

The interior of the ship was magnificent. The floors were covered in soft, thick carpet. The walls were tastefully painted.

"If the hallways are like this," said Diona. "What's the rest of the ship like?"

No one appeared to march them away to the dungeons, so they ventured forward. They turned toward a door off the hallway. It slid open and they entered.

It was a small recreation room, but nothing like the one on *Providus*. This was luxurious. There were

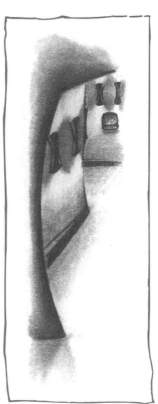

astrorecliner chairs. There was a music library containing thousands of discs. There were books in audio and video format. There was also a large collection of paper books protected behind glass doors. Juliana gasped with pleasure. She sat down in one of the astrorecliners. It fitted itself to her shape.

They found a large dining hall with enough plates, glasses, and cutlery for an army. In the kitchen area, there were freezers and cupboards full of food.

"Where is everybody?" asked Juliana. "I feel like Goldilocks."

"I'm hungry," said Diona. None of them had eaten for a long time.

"Diona, why don't you and Bogdan stay here with Astrid and have something to eat," said Sage. "Juliana and I will look around."

They seemed to be on the operations level. The rooms were full of equipment to keep every aspect of the spaceship working. They found the bridge from where the captain would have directed the ship.

"Look," said Sage. "There's a transceiver."

"Is it working?" asked Juliana.

"I think so."

"We can send a message to Earth."

"But will they reply? They've already decided we're not worth rescuing." Sage sat down at the console.

"Do you know how to work it?" Juliana asked.

"Yes. But I don't know the ISA code. It was programmed in on the *Providus*."

"Can't we just send out a Mayday signal?"

Sage examined the transceiver settings. "It's set automatically to a code, but I don't know where the message will go."

"It must be the pirates' headquarters on Earth or a secret base on some other planet," said Juliana.

"If they get a message from some kids on their huge, expensive ship, they might send someone to get us."

"What can we do? Did you ever contact anybody else?" asked Juliana.

"Only a wriggler in Iraq."

"A what?"

"A wriggler, someone who breaks into a communications system."

"Sage, were you allowed to fool around on the transceiver?"

"Of course not. But I had fun. Mostly I came across people once and never heard from them again. Wrigglers don't usually give out their codes in case someone tracks them down and arrests them. This guy, Hassan, was really cool. We kept in touch for a while."

"Can you remember his code?"

"I think so. It's a long shot." Sage wiped his sweaty hands on his pants.

"What should I say?"

compose: *To write or create.*

They composed and recomposed the message several

times before they were happy with it. "We are survivors from *Providus*. Scientists all injured during solar flares and in life-support cocoons. We require assistance." Sage then listed all their names. He hit the send key.

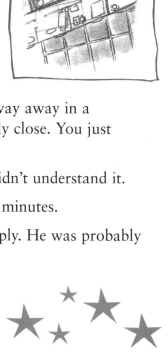

"That's it. It's gone."

"How long will it take to get there?"

"It'll be there already."

"It's hard to believe anything could travel so far in such a short time."

"It hasn't traveled that far. Wormholes are shortcuts, where the universe folds back on itself. Places that are a long way away in a straight line are actually relatively close. You just jump the gap."

Juliana shook her head. She didn't understand it.

They waited. They waited ten minutes.

"He's had plenty of time to reply. He was probably arrested a long time ago."

"Are you sure you got the code right?"

"Not really."

Juliana sighed. It would have been nice to hear from someone else in the universe. "Don't tell the others that we tried to use the transceiver. Let's finish looking around."

Sage and Juliana spent two hours searching and found no one. It would take weeks to investigate the whole ship. Memory of the food eventually forced them to give up and return to the dining hall.

"There's nobody here," said Juliana as she tucked into a large bowl of soup. "The ship is empty."

"You couldn't have looked everywhere," said Diona.

"No, but there's no one on this level, and this is where everything happens."

"We found the bridge. It was deserted."

"I accessed a plan of the ship," said Sage. "This is the operations level. The one below us is the crew quarters and other recreational areas. Below that, the other levels are all cargo areas."

"Where did the pirates go?"

"Perhaps they knew something we don't know. Perhaps this ship's about to explode or be hit by a comet."

"There are no alarms going off, no warning lights flashing."

"Now what do we do?"

"Sleep."

Sage led them to an elevator. The next level was even more luxurious than the parts of the ship they had already seen. There were whole rooms for different leisure activities: surround screens for watching videos, tennis courts, golf tees. There was a pool for swimming that was almost as big as *Providus*.

Each crew member had a separate apartment to live in. Juliana was investigating the contents of a wardrobe. There were neat uniforms as well as pretty dresses made of expensive fabric.

"This isn't the sort of thing I thought pirates would wear," she said, holding out a dress covered with sparkling discs.

"Did you think they all had beards and eye patches?"

"I thought they were all grubby men."

"Lots of pirates used to be in the military or

worked for space corporations," Bogdan told them. "When the wars ended and mining the planets stopped, they were out of work. Many of them turned to piracy."

"But I didn't expect them to have wives."

"Or children," said Diona, finding toys in a closet.

"You're still thinking that pirates have to be male," said Bogdan. "Plenty of space pirates are women."

"You seem to know a lot about them," said Juliana.

"I did a school assignment on pirates."

"So how come you didn't know about this place?"

"It's probably a secret, Diona," said Sage. "Let's get some sleep."

Some of the sleeping quarters were big enough for crew members and their families. They chose an apartment with enough beds for them all. The pirate ship might have been comfortable, but it was still spooky. No one wanted to be alone.

As they settled down to sleep, Diona asked the question they had all been wondering.

"Where are the pirates?"

"They must have gone somewhere."

"There's an explanation," said Bogdan. "I've already started to collect information. I'll figure out what happened to them."

"It's a big ship," said Diona. "Maybe they're all on deck 43 taking inventory or doing a spring cleaning." She glanced nervously at the door. "They might show up at any moment, like the three bears."

"What do you think happened to them, Bogdan?" asked Juliana.

"They could have all been called away to a big salvage job and had a fatal accident."

"There's no use guessing," said Sage. "Go to sleep."

O ver the next few days, they got used to the fact that they were the only people on the huge ship. Everyone chose their own quarters. They moved their parents' life-support cocoons onto the pirate ship. They learned how to find their way around. They found communication bugs to pin to their collars, so that no one got lost on the vast ship.

They discovered the games room.

> **take inventory**: To list all the things on hand or in view.

It was crammed full of the best games and the most advanced holograph equipment Sage had ever seen. There was a music room with all kinds of electronic equipment, as well as a beautiful rosewood grand piano. Everyone settled down to a pleasant, comfortable life of luxury.

Bogdan worked on finding out what had happened to the pirates. He happily spent his time sitting in front of screens, accessing data. Diona kept coming up with bizarre theories about the missing pirates. They had flown into a cloud of poison gas that had made them crazy and caused them to jump out into space. Then an alien space monster had come and eaten them all. Bogdan ignored her suggestions.

Juliana was more restless. She investigated the cargo decks. Each one was crammed with spaceships, satellites, probes, mining drones, every kind of spacecraft ever made.

Juliana called a meeting.

"Is this it? Is this what you plan to do for the rest of your lives? Just lounge around."

"Can't you just relax, Jules?" asked Sage. "We could have died. We've survived. I think we're entitled to take things easy for a while." He put on his games mask.

"What about our parents? Are you just going to leave them in cocoons forever?"

"It's too risky to try to revive them. Even with the equipment on board this ship. They need doctors."

Juliana sighed. She wanted to do something, but she didn't know what.

"We could take this ship to Earth," said Diona casually.

Juliana looked up at Diona. "What did you say?"

"The ship isn't damaged at all, is it? Why can't we fly it to Earth?"

The thought stunned them all.

"Is there enough fuel?" asked Juliana.

"Probably," said Bogdan. "The ship has its own nuclear reactor."

Sage took off his games mask. "Do you have any idea how complicated this ship is? It takes

> **nuclear reactor:** A device used to create power with nuclear energy.

six years of training to fly a standard ISA ship. This one is a million times more advanced."

"We've got plenty of time. How hard can it be?"

"Very, very hard."

"We need someone to teach us."

"Who did you have in mind? The pirates have disappeared into thin air."

Juliana was determined not to let go of this idea. She went up to the control room and looked at the walls of equipment, the rows of screens all showing different readouts.

If no one else would do it, she would do it herself. It might take half her life, but she would get over her fear of technology. Whoever had piloted this ship had once been as ignorant as she. They had started from scratch and learned how it all worked. Would it be possible for her to learn? She didn't want to spend the rest of her life playing games.

A movement behind the console made her jump. She was expecting to see a pirate. It was Bogdan.

"Gosh! You scared me."

"I was checking the messages received just before

the pirates disappeared," he said.

"Find anything interesting?"

"Yes, I think I have."

Sage entered the control room.

"Yes, Bogdan," he said. "What did you find?"

"It seems there was a mutiny."

"What's a mutiny?" asked Diona, who had come to see where everyone was.

"They dumped the captain and the officers. Then they sent them off in a spaceship by themselves. From what I can tell from the flight log, there was no one left who really knew how to fly the ship."

"I've been reading about how the ship works," said Sage. "It's pretty much automatic. The hard thing is plotting the course. It has to be exact. You have to know where every asteroid and comet will be years from now."

"That's exactly what they didn't know. I think one of them tried to navigate it and thought they were heading for Alpha Centauri C, the red dwarf. When they realized they weren't, they panicked and abandoned ship."

mutiny: A rebellion against people in charge.

"So where are they?"

Bogdan shrugged. Even he didn't have all the answers.

One of the screens was beeping and flashing. Juliana looked closer. A flashing sign said "Incoming Message." She followed the on-screen instructions and accessed the message.

"It's from the ISA."

They gathered around and read the message.

"Received message relayed through illegal channels. The people of Earth rejoice that you are alive. Your example of international cooperation is inspiring. A cease-fire has been called in the war between New Euro and UAS. Rescue mission will be launched as soon as possible."

"Wow, did they call off a war because of us?"

"Sounds like it."

"Hassan must have received our message and relayed it to the ISA."

"What message?" asked Diona. "Who's Hassan?"

"Send a message back, Sage," said Juliana. "Tell them we don't need a rescue mission."

"Are you serious?" They were all gaping at her.

"Yes. Tell them all we need are instructions on how

to fly this thing. Tell them we'll be bringing back billions of dollars worth of stolen spacecraft and equipment."

Sage smiled and nodded. "Jules is right. We've come this far, we can get to Earth by ourselves."

"We can, we can do it," said Juliana. She truly believed they could. Juliana had learned to trust in herself and in the others. They had each contributed something, even Astrid when she had "drawn" the Scooter. And they weren't alone anymore. Everyone on Earth knew about them. They all wanted them to return safely.

Sage sent the message. Within a few minutes there was an answer. The ISA had an agent who knew how to operate the pirate ship. Instructions would be sent.

"We're going to Earth!" said Diona, laughing and crying at the same time.

Juliana laughed, too. She had a future again.

Space Facts

Alpha is the first letter of the Greek alphabet. In astronomy, alpha is usually the name given to the brightest star in a constellation. A constellation is a group of stars.

Alpha Centauri is the closest solar system to our own. This system has three suns. Two of the suns are orbiting each other. They are so close together that to us they look like just one star.

The stars have fascinated humans for centuries. The first astronomers were the Babylonians. They recorded the first astronomical observations in 747 B.C.—they recorded how often solar eclipses happened.

Scientists in spaceships study celestial bodies. They also carry out experiments related to weightlessness and the growth patterns of living things in space.

A galaxy is a cluster of stars, dust, and gas held together by gravity. There are 200 billion stars in the Milky Way galaxy.

Radiation suits protect the wearer from the effects of radioactive energy.

Spacecraft of today, like the Galileo probe, can travel at speeds of between 25,000 to 37,000 mph.

Traveling at the speed of a space shuttle, it would take about twelve hours to reach the moon from Earth. It would take around twenty-eight weeks to reach the sun. But it would take almost 150,000 years to reach the closest star to Earth.

Where to from Here?

You've just read the story of Juliana and her friends in outer space. Here are some ideas for finding out more about the world of science fiction.

The Library

Some books you might enjoy include:
- *The Ear, The Eye, and the Arm*, by Nancy Farmer
- *The Egypt Game,* by Zilpha Kealtey Snyder
- *The Giver,* by Lois Lowry
- *A Wrinkle in Time,* by Madeleine L'Engle

Here's a nonfiction book to try:
- *Adventure in Space: The Flight to Fix the Hubble,* by Elaine Scott and Margaret Miller

TV, Film, and Video

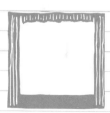

Check TV listings and ask about other science fiction films at a video store or at your library.
- *Star Trek* episodes
- *The Twilight Zone*
- The *Star Wars* movies
- *E.T.: The Extraterrestrial*

The Internet

Try searches using key words, such as *science fiction, space, space travel,* and *robotics.*

Also check *www.nasa.gov* for facts about the U.S. space program and missions.

People and Places

If there is a science museum nearby, visit and ask questions. Look for other sources, such as science fiction magazines for young people.

The Ultimate Nonfiction Book

Be sure to check out *Real Sci-Fi,* the companion volume to *Out of Orbit. Real Sci-Fi* tells you about some other amazing things, such as robots that were once science fiction and are now real.

Decide for yourself where fiction stops and fact begins.